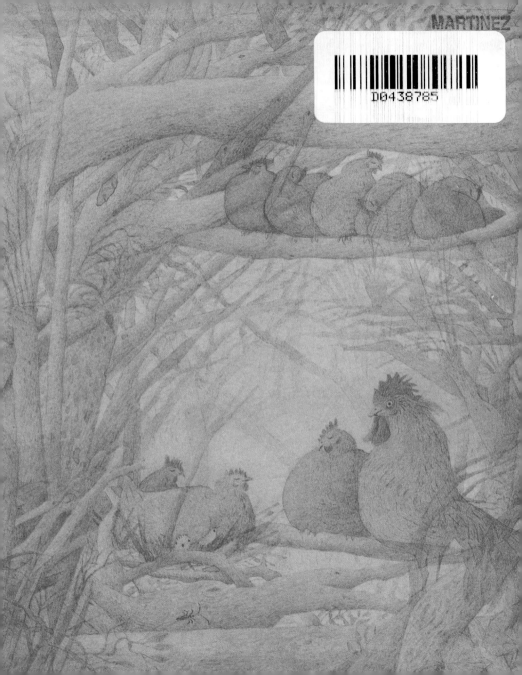

Henrietta

and the

Golden Eggs

Käthi Bhend

pictures

translated by John Barrett

Hanna Johansen

Henrietta
and the
Golden Eggs

David R. Godine · *Publisher* · *Boston*

Once upon a time

there were

three thousand three hundred

and thirty-three chickens

who lived in a great, big chicken house

on a chicken farm.

5

The air stank

of chicken droppings and fortified chicken feed.

There was a lot of pushing and shoving

on the ground, because each chicken
had just enough room for its feet,
but no more.

Things were not going well
for the three thousand three hundred
and thirty-three chickens.
Many of them had a cough
and almost all of them were losing feathers
because they pecked at one another
whenever they stepped
on each other's feet.

The chickens laid an egg
almost every day.
When they were done,
they gave a loud cluck
to let the other chickens know
who had laid the egg.
And every day
the manager counted up the eggs
that his three thousand three hundred
and thirty-three chickens
had laid.

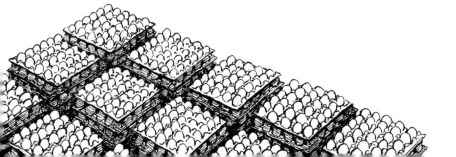

Among the chickens, there was one
who was still little.
Henrietta was waiting
for the time when
she would be a big chicken
and could lay an egg every day.
Henrietta said,
"When I'm big,
I'm going to lay golden eggs."

"Hahahaha!" said the big chickens.
"Golden eggs!"
Then they needed to cough.

Because Henrietta was so little
and the time had not yet come
for her to lay eggs,
she said,
"But first I'm going to learn to sing."

"Don't even bother trying,"
said the big chickens.

"Well I'm going to try anyway,"
said little Henrietta.

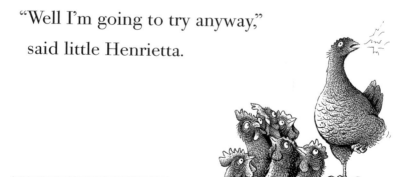

Then she looked around

in the chicken house

until she found a place in the corner

where she could peck and scratch.

And she pecked and scratched

until she had scratched open a hole.

The hole was small

but when Henrietta

put her eye to it,

she could see something green

on the other side.

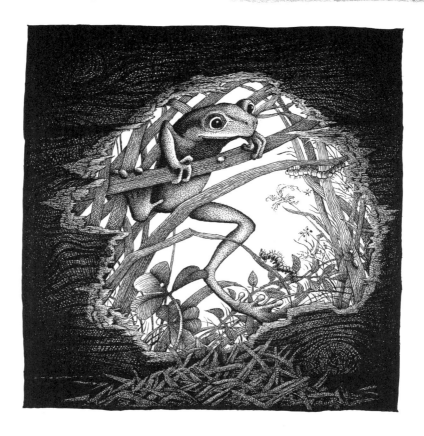

Henrietta had never seen
anything green.
Everything that Henrietta knew about
was red or brown
or yellow or gray
and at night everything was black.
Henrietta went on pecking.
Every day the hole got bigger.
Henrietta pecked and scratched
until the hole was big enough
for her to slip through.

She could do that because she was so little.

How different everything was
outside the chicken house!
There was fresh air everywhere
and it didn't smell of chicken droppings
or fortified chicken feed anywhere.
When Henrietta
had gotten accustomed to
the brightness,
she saw
that things outside
were not only green
but blue as well.

Then Henrietta came to a wheat field
where she could run around and peck
and scratch and cluck
as much as she wanted to.
Just as it was getting dark,
Henrietta slipped back inside
with the other three thousand three hundred
and thirty-three chickens
in the chicken house.

Every day Henrietta made
the hole a little bit bigger.
Then she went out into the wheat field
to sing.
Henrietta clucked and clucked
until one day she thought,
"Now I've practiced enough.
Now I can sing."

"You call that singing?"
said the big chickens.

But that day
the hole had become big enough
for the big chickens.
They all slipped out into the open,
one after another,
three thousand three hundred
and thirty-three chickens.

And then they ran
into the wheat field
and pecked
and scratched
and clucked for joy.

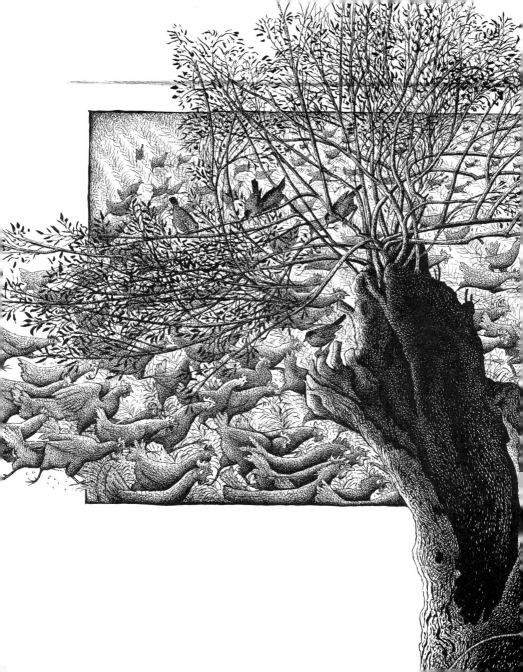

"Just look at this mess!"
  screamed the manager.
"The chickens are in the wheat field!"
  There were, of course,
  three thousand three hundred
  and thirty-three chickens there.
  And when the manager
  sent his workers out
  to round them all up,
  the chickens ran
  this way and that way
  and it took the whole day
  to get them all locked in again.

And then they sat
in their chicken house
in their chicken smell
and pulled each other's feathers out
and coughed.

Henrietta was the only one
who didn't have a cough.

And the hole in the corner
was closed up.

Then Henrietta said once more,
"When I'm big,
   I'm going to lay golden eggs."

"Hahahaha!"
   coughed the big chickens.

"But first I'm going to learn to swim,"
   said Henrietta.

"Don't even bother trying,"
   said the big chickens.

"Well, I'm going to try anyway,"
said Henrietta.

Then she went over to the corner
and pecked and scratched
until she had pecked
the hole open again,
and she went out
into the wheat field
and over to the duck pond.

She could do that because she was so little.

She breathed the fresh air,
and scratched in the fresh earth,
and drank the fresh water,
as much as she wanted to.
And once every day
she stuck her feet into the water.

"You call that swimming?"
said the big chickens.

"The water is too wet
for my tummy,"
said Henrietta.

And then came the day
when the hole was once again big enough
for the big chickens.
They ran into the wheat field
and over to the duck pond
and pecked and scratched
and clucked for happiness.

"This is just too much!"
screamed the manager.

There were, you see,
three thousand three hundred
and thirty-three chickens,
and when the manager
sent his workers out
to round them all up,
the chickens ran
this way and that way
and it took the whole day
to get them all locked in again.

Then they sat in their chicken house,
in their chicken smell
and pulled each other's feathers out
and coughed.

Henrietta was the only one
who didn't have a cough.

And the hole in the corner
was closed up.

Then Henrietta said once again,
"When I'm big,
I'm going to lay
golden eggs."

"Hahahaha!"
  cou-haha-oughed the big chickens.

"But first I'm going to learn to fly,"
  said Henrietta.

"Don't even bother trying,"
  said the big chickens.

"Well, I'm going to try anyway,"
  said Henrietta.

Then she pecked
and scratched until
she had scratched the hole open again,
and she went into the wheat field
and over to the duck pond
and up onto the manure pile.

She could do that because she was so little.

She pecked in the fresh earth
and breathed in the fresh air
and drank the fresh water.
And every day she jumped off the manure pile
into the air as high as she could,
flapping her wings all the while.

"You call that flying?"

said the big chickens.

And then came the day
when the hole was big enough for everyone.
Henrietta made a clucking noise
and led all
three thousand three hundred
and thirty-three chickens
out into the open,
into the wheat field,
over to the duck pond,
and up onto the manure pile.

And they had a big celebration.

When the manager
sent his workers out again
to round up the chickens
they couldn't do it.
The chickens ran away too quickly,
this way and that way,
and kept finding
new places to hide,
so that in the evening
the workers said, "We can't
catch them all today.
We'll finish tomorrow."

The next day
was no different.
Nor was the third day.
And so, on the evening of the third day
the workers said
to the manager,

"There are three thousand three hundred
and thirty-three chickens,
and it's impossible
to round them all up again,
if they don't want to be caught."

"This is a catastrophe!"
  screamed the manager.
"We have to have eggs to sell."

"No,
  it's not a catastrophe,"
  said the workers.
"If we build a great, big, chicken yard
  out here in the open
  for all three thousand three hundred
  and thirty-three chickens,
  it'll all work out."

And that's just what they did.

From then on, the chickens
could go out into the open every day.
They clucked and scratched and pecked
as much as they wanted to.
At night they slept
on the roosts in the coop.
They laid their eggs in their new nests.
And the manager
sent his workers out
to gather the eggs.
Soon the chickens began to grow new feathers,
and not one of them
had a cough any longer.

In the meantime
Henrietta had grown as big
as the big chickens
and the day finally
came for Henrietta
to lay her first egg.

The three thousand three hundred
and thirty-three chickens
watched with interest.
"Now we'll just see
whether it's a golden egg."

Henrietta sat on her nest

and pushed her

first egg out.

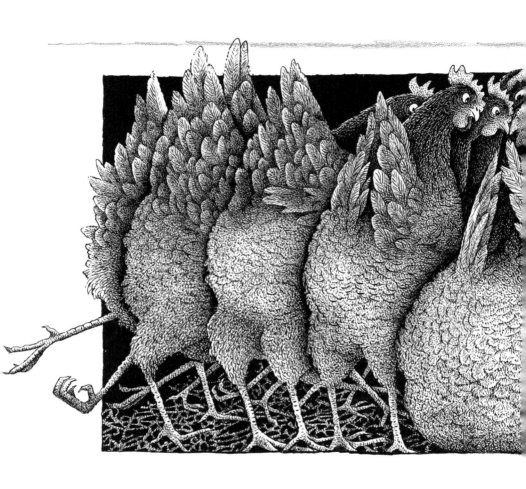

And when it finally lay there, it was
a beautiful ...

smooth ... round ... bright ...

brown egg.

"Look!"
said the chickens,
"it's not a golden egg after all!
You didn't even need
to bother trying."

And what did Henrietta do?

Henrietta laughed at all of them
and said,
"Did you *really* believe
that a chicken
could lay golden eggs?"

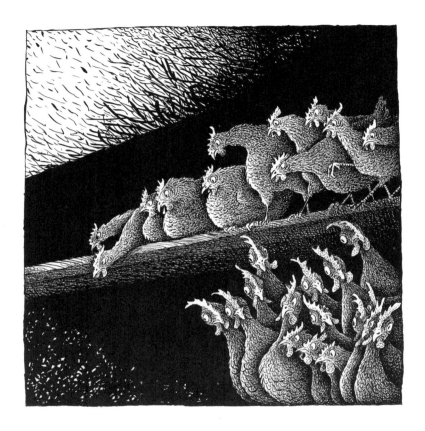

First U.S. edition published in 2002 by
David R. Godine, Publisher
Post Office Box 450
Jaffrey, New Hampshire 03542
www.godine.com

Originally published in German as
Vom Hühnchen das goldene Eier legen wollte

Copyright © 1998 by Verlag Nagel & Kimche AG, Zürich/Frauenfeld
Translation copyright © 2002 by John S. Barrett

LIBRARY OF CONGRESS CATALOGING-IN-PUBLICATION DATA

Johansen, Hanna, 1939–
[Vom Hühnchen das goldene Eier legen wollte. English]
Henrietta and the golden eggs / Hanna Johansen ;
Käthi Bhend, pictures. – 1st. U.S. ed.
p. cm.
Summary: The persistence of Henrietta, one of 3,333 chickens
on a chicken farm, leads to a better life for them all.
ISBN 1–56792–210–4 (alk. paper)
[1. Chickens–Fiction. 2. Persistence–Fiction. 3. Farm life–Fiction.]
I. Bhend, Käthi, ill. II. Title.
PZ7.J617 He 2002
[E]–dc21   2002013477

Composition and layout by Carl W. Scarbrough

FIRST U.S. EDITION
Printed in Canada